A Symphony for the Sheep

written by
C. M. Millen

illustrated by
Mary Azarian

Houghton Mifflin Company Boston 1996

For information about this and other Houghton Mifflin
trade and reference books and multimedia products,
visit The Bookstore at Houghton Mifflin on the World
Wide Web at http://www.hmco.com/trade/.

Manufactured in the United States of America

Book design by David Saylor
The text of this book is set in 16-point Caxton Book.
The illustrations are hand-colored woodcuts,
reproduced in full color.

HOR   10   9   8   7   6   5   4   3   2   1

Library of Congress Cataloging-in-Publication Data
Millen, C. M.
A symphony for the sheep / C. M. Millen ;
illustrated by Mary Azarian
p. cm.
Summary: After the shearer removes the winter coat
from the sheep, the spinner, weaver, and knitter,
each in turn, do their part to produce the wool sweater.
ISBN 0-395-76503-X
[1. Sheep-shearing—Fiction. 2. Wool—Fiction.
3. Stories in rhyme.] I. Azarian, Mary, ill. II. Title.
PZ8.3.M6115Sy 1996 [E]—dc20
95-43097   CIP   AC

In the spring when ewes are lambing
and the rams do watchful stand

come the days of gentle warming,
longer light on softer land.

Gone are meaner, darker days
when, in winter's bitter lair,
sheep do blossom wooly capes
to shield them from the icy air.

Now the shearer comes around
to shave away their curly coats
and take the greasy wool to town
for use by nimble Ulster folk.

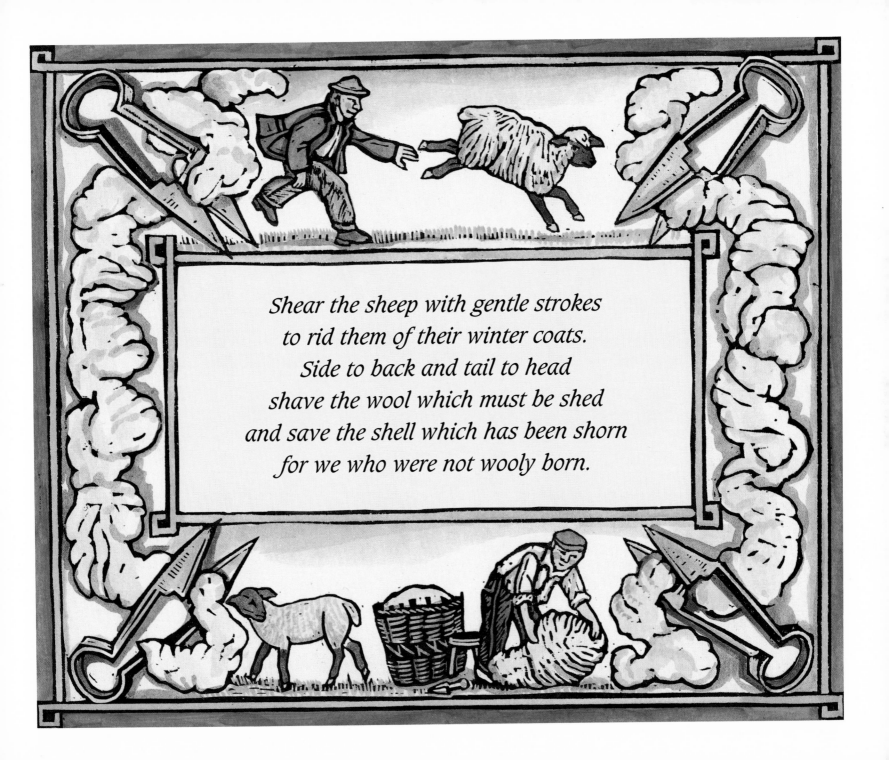

Shear the sheep with gentle strokes
to rid them of their winter coats.
Side to back and tail to head
shave the wool which must be shed
and save the shell which has been shorn
for we who were not wooly born.

The spinner keeps a steady beat
upon the treadle with her feet
as through her nimble fingers slides
the greasy wool which she must glide
into the soft and steady strands
for use by other nimble hands.
And so it goes and so it comes—
the spinner's work is never done.

The shearer keeps her well supplied
with wooly coats the sheep provide
which must be washed and must be carded
well before the spinning's started.

After which the skeins are weighed
and hung aloft to set them straight.
And so it goes and so it comes—
there's always wool which must be spun.

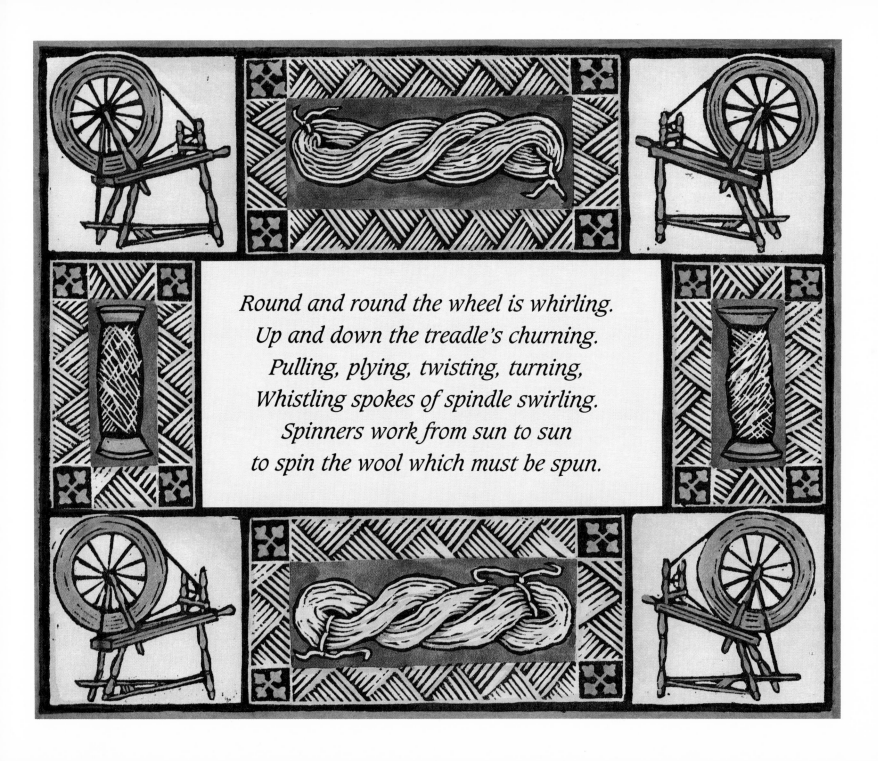

Round and round the wheel is whirling.
Up and down the treadle's churning.
Pulling, plying, twisting, turning,
Whistling spokes of spindle swirling.
Spinners work from sun to sun
to spin the wool which must be spun.

In Donegal
we weave the wool
with warp
and weft
upon the loom.

The shuttle flies
and colors bloom
in blues and greens of stormy seas
against a sky of weathered grey
and muted hues of heathered heaths
which climb the hills of Derryveagh.

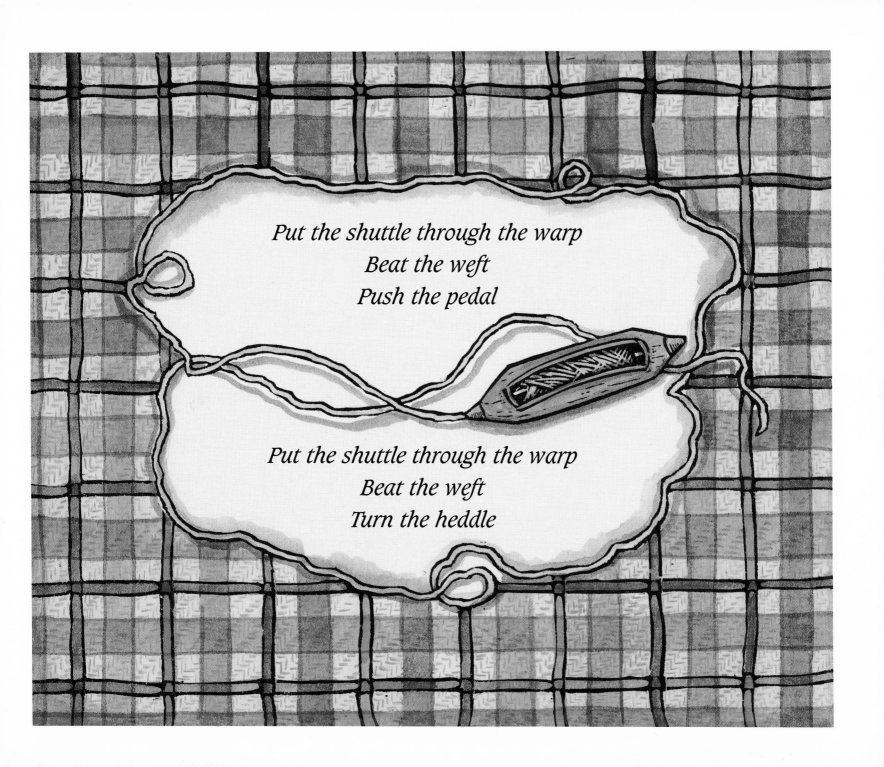

Put the shuttle through the warp
Beat the weft
Push the pedal

Put the shuttle through the warp
Beat the weft
Turn the heddle

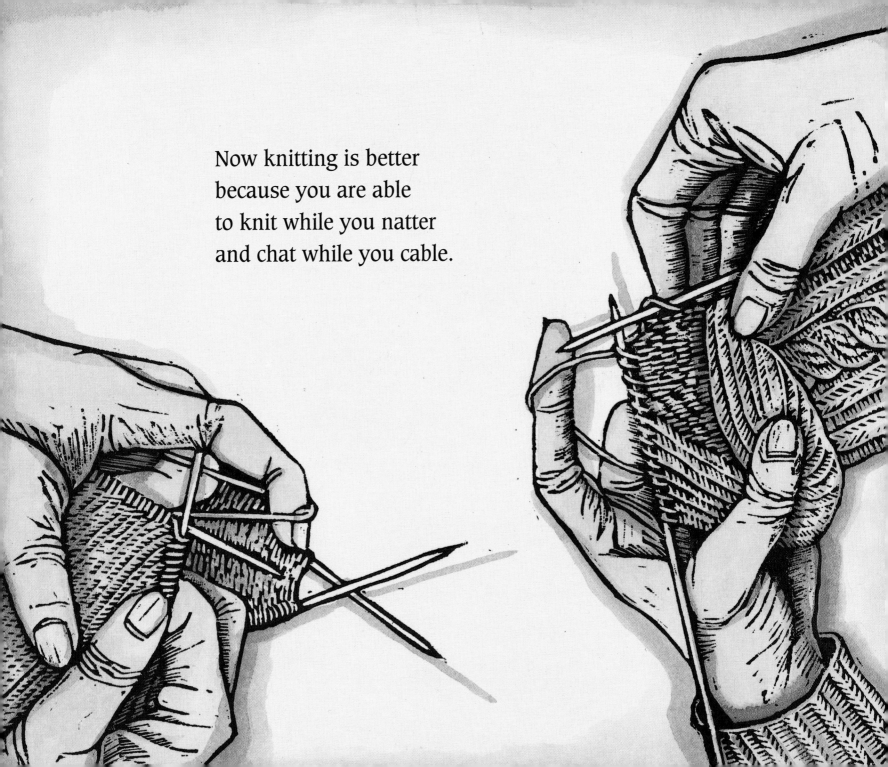

Now knitting is better
because you are able
to knit while you natter
and chat while you cable.

While weavers are loners
and spinners keep quiet
two knitters together
can make quite a riot

and several can gather
together and blather
while outfitting sweaters
that outwit the weather.

Which might be the reason
that in every season
as rain fills the sky
Irish wit remains dry!

Knitters chat and knit
chat and knit
chat and knit and natter.
Knitters chat and slip
chat and knit
chat and purl.

Shear the sheep with gentle strokes
to rid them of their winter coats.
Side to back and tail to head
shave the wool which must be shed
and save the shell which has been shorn
for we who were not wooly born.

Round and round the wheel is whirling.
Up and down the treadle's churning.
Pulling, plying, twisting, turning,
Whistling spokes of spindle swirling.
Spinners work from sun to sun
to spin the wool which must be spun.

Put the shuttle through the warp
Beat the weft
Push the pedal
Put the shuttle through the warp
Beat the weft
Turn the heddle

Knitters chat and knit
chat and knit
chat and knit and natter.
Knitters chat and slip
chat and knit
chat and purl.

A Note from the Author

In poetry, words, like notes of varying beats, come together to create melodies. And, just as in a song, the melodies of the phrases contribute as much to the meaning of a poem as the words themselves. In *A Symphony for the Sheep,* the poem is told in four parts: the shearer, the spinner, the weaver, and the knitter. Each part has a refrain—the stanza which has the border around it—which was written to represent the melody of the action being described. You can hear the rhythm of the shearing, the spinning, the weaving, and the knitting as you speak the words.

Another way to hear the "music" in this book is to divide the poem up among four readers, each reader taking one of the four parts. After you've all read the poem through to the end, have the shearer read his refrain repeatedly, with the other readers joining in sequentially, as in a round. By the time the knitter joins in, all four readers will be reading simultaneously, each maintaining the individual rhythm of his refrain, yet together making a four-part poetic harmony—*A Symphony for the Sheep!*　　　—C. M. M.